The Children's Aesop

Selected Fables

RETOLD BY

Stephanie Calmenson

ILLUSTRATED BY

Robert Byrd

DOUBLEDAY BOOK & MUSIC CLUBS, INC., GARDEN CITY, NEW YORK

To Rachel Cole

Art direction by Diana Klemin
Designed by November and Lawrence, Inc.
Text and illustrations copyright © 1988 by Doubleday Book & Music Clubs, Inc.
All Rights Reserved
Printed in the United States of America
3 4 5 6 7 8 9 10

CONTENTS

The Hare and the Tortoise

One day, Hare was bragging loudly to the circle of animals who had gathered round him. "Not only am I handsome," said Hare, "but I am *fast!* No one is faster than I!"

At that moment, Tortoise came along and broke into the circle. "You may be fast, Hare" said Tortoise quietly, "but I would like to race you. I am sure that I will win."

Hare threw back his head and laughed. "Why, you are the slowest thing on four feet, Tortoise. How could you possibly win a race with me?"

"Will you let me try?" Tortoise asked.

Hare agreed to the race. The other animals set the course to be run and made a starting line.

Fox was chosen to start the race. "On your mark. Get set. Go!" she said.

Hare took off at top speed, leaving Tortoise in the dust. He looked back to see Tortoise growing smaller and smaller in the distance. When he could see no sign of Tortoise at all, Hare stopped running.

"What a silly creature Tortoise is, to think that he could win this race. It was nice of me to agree to it, but there's no need to tire myself out. I think I'll just stop here for a little nap."

With that, Hare went off the road to a grassy spot, leaned back against a rock and closed his eyes.

Meantime, Tortoise plodded on at his own steady pace. Hare was nowhere in sight, but Tortoise was not worried. "I'll just do my best," thought Tortoise. It wasn't long before he passed Hare.

When Hare woke up from his nap, he yawned and stretched. "Now, what am I doing here?" he wondered aloud. "Ah, yes, I am racing. Racing with Tortoise." He chuckled at the thought, then continued down the road toward the finish line.

Hare looked behind him, but saw no sign of Tortoise. This time he should have been looking ahead. For as soon as he turned the bend he found Tortoise, on the winning side of the finish line, resting in the shade of a big oak tree.

SLOW BUT STEADY WINS THE RACE.

The Dog and His Bone

There once was a Dog known for being foolish and greedy. Listen to his story and you will know why:

One day, Dog was trotting along proudly with a large bone in his mouth.

"It was nice of that butcher to give me this bone," said Dog. "I can't wait to get home and start chewing it!"

Just then, Dog came to a plank of wood set across a running stream. As he was crossing, he looked down and saw another Dog that looked very much like himself. This Other Dog was holding an even larger bone in his mouth.

Dog began to growl. "What makes you so special to have a bigger bone than mine. Does the butcher like you better?"

With that Dog dropped his bone down into the stream and plunged in after the Other Dog. But there really was no Other Dog. Dog had been looking at his own reflection. There was no larger bone either. That had been a reflection too.

Dog slapped his paws against the water in frustration. Then he climbed out of the stream and went home with no bone at all.

That is Dog's story. Now you know why he is called foolish and greedy, don't you?

IF YOU RISK WHAT YOU HAVE ONLY TO GET MORE, YOU MAY END UP WITH NOTHING.

The Fox Who Lost

Once, a poor Fox got caught in a hunter's trap. In order to free himself, he had to cut off his own tail. The Fox healed, but of course his tail never grew back.

"I can't let the others know that I have lost my tail," said the Fox to himself. "They'll laugh at me!"

So he went into hiding. The Fox stayed hidden for many days and nights, deep in thought. Finally he came out, and called a meeting of all foxes. When they had gathered, the Fox made sure his back was in the shadows. Then he stood up tall, took a deep breath, and said:

"Fellow foxes! I have called this meeting to speak to you on the subject of tails. Don't you know how silly you look with those long, bushy things? Besides being unsightly, they slow you down, making

His Tail

you easy targets for hunters. Those tails are good for nothing except trouble. Cut them off, I say! Get rid of them!"

The crowd gasped! Was this Fox serious? Were their tails really that awful?

While they were studying the matter, the Oldest Fox sneaked around the crowd into the shadows. He came back shaking his head sadly.

"Pay no attention to this Fox," he said. "He is not speaking for your good. You see, he lost his own tail. That is the only reason he does not want you to keep yours."

"Yes," said the others. "Now we understand."

MISERY LOVES COMPANY.

The Crow and the Pitcher

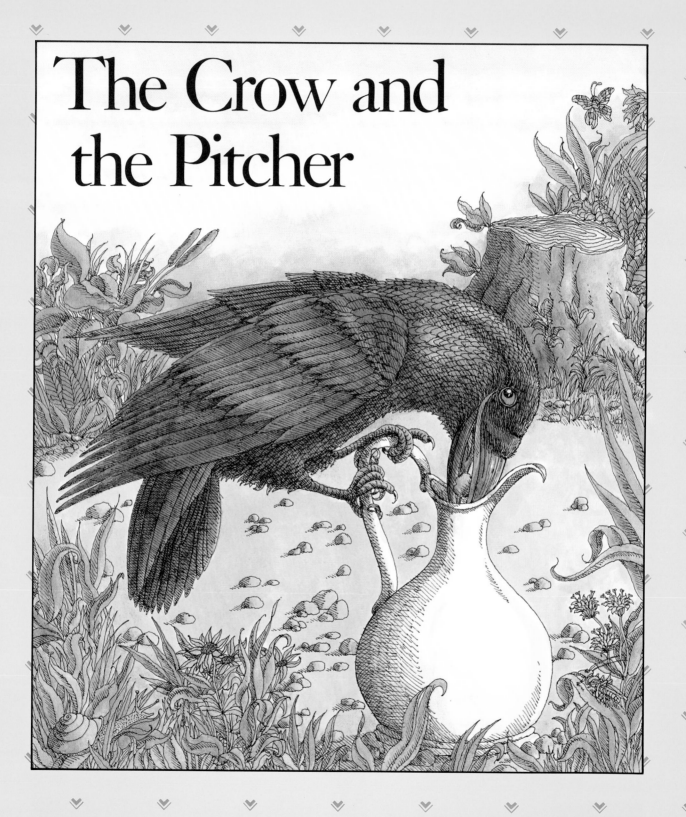

Once a thirsty Crow flying overhead was lucky enough to spot a pitcher sitting by the roadside. As she came in for a landing, she imagined the great gulps of cool water that awaited her. But the Crow was not as lucky as she had hoped. She dipped her beak into the pitcher's narrow neck and came up dry. Then she cocked her head and peeked down into the pitcher to find that there was only a little water at the very bottom. Since the neck was so narrow, there was no easy way to get to the water.

"All right," said the Crow, gathering her wits. "If there is water in the pitcher, there is a way to get at it."

The Crow paced up and down beside the pitcher and began a long conversation with herself.

"I could knock the pitcher over and try to drink the water before it falls into the dirt," Crow said to herself.

"Bad idea, Crow," she answered. "There's no way to get to that water fast enough."

Crow tried again. "I could fly off to a town somewhere and find a straw."

"Sure thing," Crow said to herself. "By the time I get back, five smarter birds will have had their fill."

Crow found herself pacing so fast that she was all tired out and had to sit down to rest.

"Ouch!" cried Crow when she hit the pebbles that lay on the ground. "That hurts."

Crow jumped back up, but not without a new idea.

"Crow, you are a very smart bird!" she said to herself. One by one, she picked up the pebbles and dropped them down the narrow neck of the pitcher. Just as she thought, the water rose higher and higher as the pebbles took the water's place at the bottom. Finally, the water was close enough to the top so that Crow could dip her beak in and enjoy her well-deserved drink.

NECESSITY IS THE MOTHER OF INVENTION.

The Ant and the Grasshopper

Grasshopper loved summer. She liked to sit in the bright, warm sun singing the hours away. "Tra-la-la-la, tra-la-la-lee!" she sang merrily.

Ant loved summer, too. But she knew better than to sit around singing. She knew that summer would not last forever, and when winter arrived there would be no food around. So she worked hard gathering corn to store for the cold months ahead.

"You're so busy!" chuckled Grasshopper. "Why don't you sit awhile and enjoy my songs."

"Take my advice," said Ant. "If singing is all you do now, you'll be sorry later."

But Grasshopper wouldn't listen. She sang all summer long and right into autumn. Before she knew it, winter came rushing in.

Grasshopper was in trouble. She was so hungry she could hardly sing a note. "Tra-la, tra-lee," she whispered weakly. She tried to dance to keep the cold away, but finally she dropped to the ground, exhausted.

Grasshopper was lying in a heap in the snow when she saw Ant pass by with her corn. Grasshopper tried calling to Ant, but her cries for help were carried off in the cold winter wind.

"If only I had listened," thought the weary Grasshopper, "I would not be in this trouble."

PREPARE TODAY FOR THE NEEDS OF TOMORROW.

The Wind and

"I'm stronger!"

"No, *I'm* stronger!"

"No, *I* am!

The Wind and the Sun had been arguing this way for hours. Finally they decided to put their strength to the test. Whoever was able to get the coat off the next traveler to pass by would be declared the strongest.

While they waited, they continued their bickering.

"This is going to be easy," bragged the Wind. "A huff here, a puff there, and that coat will be a memory."

"You think you're such a big shot," said the Sun. "But I wouldn't get too puffed up if I were you. You see, I am sure I have the better way to get the coat off."

Just then a man with his overcoat wrapped tightly around him headed in their direction.

"You can go first," said the Sun to the Wind. And the Sun ducked

the Sun

behind a cloud to watch.

The Wind drew in his breath and blew with all his might. The coat's tail waved a little bit, but the man just hugged the coat to him closer than before. The Wind tried again and again until finally he was all tired out.

"Now it's my turn," said the Sun calmly. She grew as bright as she knew how and baked the man gently in her warm rays. Sure enough the man slowed down and then stopped altogether. He lifted his face to the Sun and held it there, smiling for a moment. Then he untied his coat and let it drop to the ground. Not only did he take off his coat, he took off all his clothes and went splashing happily in the nearby stream.

"What do you think of that?" asked the Sun.

But the Wind didn't answer. He was long gone. On top of everything, he was a sore loser.

KINDNESS WORKS BETTER THAN FORCE.

The Lion and the Mouse

Lion had been hunting all morning and was tired. He lay down in the cool grass to rest, not wanting to be disturbed. But as soon as he closed his eyes, he felt something tippy-toeing up his back.

It was a tiny, gray mouse. Lion lay as still as a rock, which is just what Mouse thought she was upon. Soon she would know better. For each step she took brought her closer to Lion's strong jaws and quick paws.

SNAP! "I've got you!" roared Lion as he whisked Mouse up by her tail. He was about to pop Mouse into his huge, hungry mouth when he heard her beg, "Please, forgive me! I did not mean to disturb you. If you will let me go this time, you can be certain I will return your kindness one day."

Lion laughed. "What could a tiny thing like you ever do for me?"

"I cannot say for sure," said Mouse. "But I promise you won't be sorry."

Lion flicked the mouse away. "You're too little to bother with anyway," he said.

A few days later, some hunters caught Lion and tied him to a tree. Mouse heard Lion's furious roar and ran to him. She quickly began gnawing through the ropes that bound him. It took some time, but finally she set Lion free.

"Thank you," said Lion. "Not only have you freed me, you have taught me a lesson worth remembering."

EVEN A SMALL FRIEND MAY BE A GREAT FRIEND.

The Stag at the Pool

A Stag was walking along one day, minding his own business, when he was startled by a magnificent sight. Reflected in a pool of water was the head of a grand animal.

"Look at those tremendous horns," said the Stag. "That is one handsome fellow!"

Some nearby birds started twittering with merriment.

"You're not very modest," said Mother Bird. "Don't you know it is your own reflection you are admiring so dearly."

The Stag would have blushed if he could. "I didn't realize," he said humbly.

He was eager to examine himself further, so he went close to the pool of water to see his whole body. Starting at the tops of his antlers, his gaze traveled down. When he got to his legs, he gasped.

"Oh, no! What measly, spindly excuses for legs!" he cried. "How can one animal have such majestic antlers and such scrawny legs? And what tiny feet I have! I'm surprised I don't fall off them and have to crawl on my belly like a snake."

While he was bemoaning his slender legs and tiny feet, the birds shouted a warning and took flight.

Stag didn't need their warning. He had already caught the scent of Lion and was on his way. The Lion was fast, but Stag's legs and feet, which had made him so unhappy before, were strong enough to carry him quickly across the open plain.

Lion would not give up, though. He chased Stag straight into the woods. And that is where Stag was undone. Upon entering the woods, Stag's antlers became entangled in the low branches of a tree. There he stood, unable to pull free, with Lion drawing dangerously near.

"How mistaken I was to curse these legs," said the Stag. "They gave me my chance at freedom. And now here I am, trapped by my antlers, which I thought were my greatest treasure."

Then all at once the Lion pounced.

TOO OFTEN WE UNDERRATE THAT WHICH IS MOST VALUABLE.

19

The Ant and the

Of course you know that Ants are very hardworking creatures. They are always going from here to there, searching for food and carrying it home.

All this hard work can make an Ant very thirsty. "It's time for my morning break!" one Ant called out to his friends. "I'll be right back." He went down to the riverside for a drink of cool water.

The Ant had just reached the river's edge when a small wave came up and carried him off.

"Help! Help!" he cried, struggling to stay afloat.

His friends did not hear him, but, fortunately, a Dove sitting up in a tree took notice. She plucked a leaf from a branch and dropped it

Dove

down toward the river. The leaf floated to the Ant, who was able to climb on it and paddle himself to shore.

The Ant was quite shaken from this experience, so he lay down to rest awhile in the grass. He was almost asleep when he heard footsteps approaching. A bird catcher clutching a net was heading straight toward the Dove's tree.

"Oh, no you don't," called the Ant fiercely. He raced to the bird catcher and bit him on the ankle. The bird catcher cried out in pain, and the Dove, hearing the cries, flew to safety.

The Ant breathed a sigh of relief. He was glad to have helped the Dove for he had always believed that . . .

ONE GOOD TURN DESERVES ANOTHER.

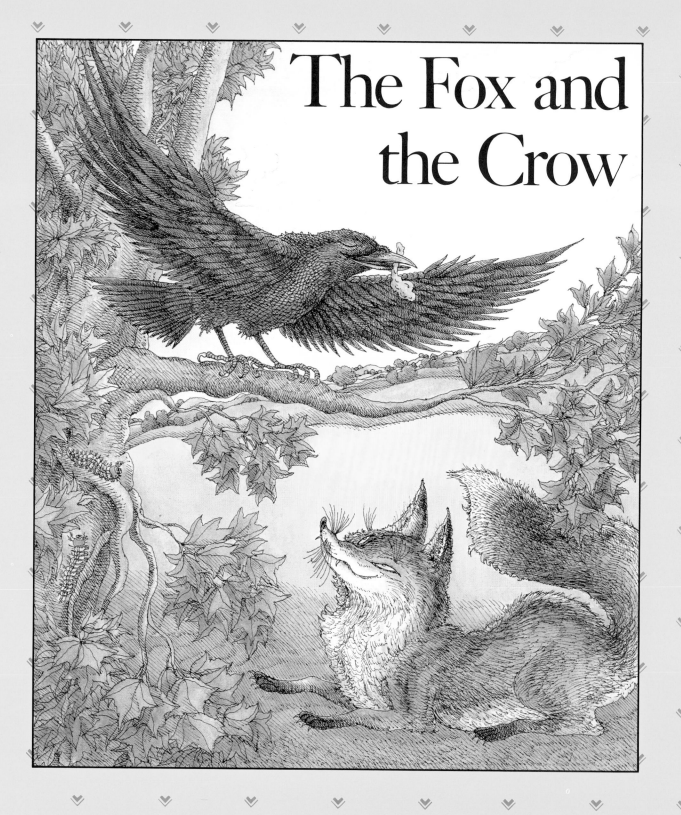

The Fox and the Crow

Fox was walking through the woods one day when he noticed Crow coming in for a landing. Crow was carrying a morsel of meat in his beak.

"That, my friends, looks like a tasty treat," thought Fox. He went and stood beneath the branch where Crow was sitting.

"Isn't it a lovely day!" Fox said, trying to start a conversation.

But Crow did not answer. He knew that the moment he opened his beak, his hard-won meal would drop into the jaws of the wily Fox. Crow thought himself much too smart to fall for a trick like that.

Fox tried again. "I was saying that it is a lovely day. But I do see a few clouds overhead. Do you think it might rain?"

Crow kept his beak shut tight.

"Well, I see you don't feel like talking today," said Fox, "but that is all right with me. I am happy just to sit here looking at you. Your feathers are so black and glossy. Your eyes are so clear and bright."

Crow was careful to keep his beak shut, but he sat up tall and spread his wings proudly.

"Yes, those are beautiful wings," continued Fox. "And I remember I once heard you sing. What a pleasure it was listening to your sweet melody. If only you would sing a note for me now!"

Crow was so excited by Fox's compliments that, without thinking, he opened his beak to sing.

"Caw! Caw! Caw!" he cried angrily as he watched the meat drop down into Fox's waiting jaws.

After gulping down the meat, Fox began to sing merrily, "Foolish Crow, didn't know! Foolish Crow, didn't know!"

And what was it foolish Crow did not know?

NEVER TRUST A FLATTERER.

The Two Pots

Two Pots were left out by a river when their owners had no more use for them. One was a strong pot made of iron, the other a weak pot made of clay.

"Fancy meeting you here," said the Pot of Iron.

"Nice to see you, too," said the Pot of Clay.

The Pots sat side by side and basked in the sunshine. Suddenly, the sky grew dark and rain came pouring down. The river rose onto the land and carried the two Pots downstream.

"Stay close by me!" shouted the Pot of Iron over the noise of the rushing water. "Together we can make it through."

"Thanks, but I think I'd be better off on my own," replied the Pot of Clay. "You see, you are my greatest danger. If we should bump together, I would break all to pieces."

"Don't worry, I'll protect you," said the Pot of Iron. He grabbed the Pot of Clay's handle. The Pot of Clay worried his way downstream. And sure enough, as they rounded the last turn, the Pot of Iron banged into his friend, the Pot of Clay, and broke him to pieces.

And so it is said:

EQUALS MAKE THE BEST FRIENDS.

The Sick Lion

Rumble, rumble, rumble.

It was Lion's stomach talking. Lion was sick and had no strength to hunt for food. But he was not about to go hungry. "If I cannot go to the food, the food must come to me!" he thought.

Lion waited until he saw a large group of animals gathered by the water hole. Then he made a big show of hobbling to his den. "Oh, oh," he moaned, "I must be dying. Come pay your last respects."

The animals talked it over among themselves and decided that since Lion was so weak, they would not be in danger. So they agreed to grant his last request.

One by one, they entered the Lion's den. Fox, who was last in line, watched as each animal disappeared.

It wasn't long before Lion was leaning back, licking his chops. "Those animals made a fine meal," he chuckled. "I should have thought of this long ago."

Then he noticed that Fox had not come in yet. "That Fox will make a tasty dessert," he said to himself.

Lion went outside and found Fox waiting there. "Won't you come in and visit with me?" Lion asked. "It could be your last chance."

"That's just what I'm afraid of," answered Fox, "for I see many footprints going into your den, but none coming out. And I notice, Lion, that you look much fuller and stronger now."

With that, Fox hurried away and she didn't look back once.

THE WISE LEARN FROM THE MISFORTUNES OF OTHERS.

The Flamingo

Early one morning, a hungry Flamingo waded into a stream for some breakfast.

She had been there only a minute when she saw a fine Trout swimming toward her. By the time the Trout realized that the Flamingo was standing there, it was too late for him to escape. But much to the Trout's surprise, the Flamingo let him pass by.

"Too small," was all the Flamingo said.

"Well, this must be my lucky day!" said the Trout happily. And he swam away.

A few minutes later, a handsome Catfish headed toward the Flamingo. He was right at the bird's feet and would easily have been captured, but the Flamingo let him pass by.

"Too bony," was all the Flamingo said.

"Well, now, I've heard cats have nine lives," thought the Catfish. "I guess they don't call me Catfish for nothing." He swam off feeling like a million dollars.

Fish after fish swam by the Flamingo. But none was good enough for her. All the Flamingo would say as she let each fish pass by was: "Too small." "Too bony." "Too ugly."

As the day wore on, the sun grew brighter overhead and the fish left the shallow part of the stream for deeper, cooler waters. The Flamingo could not follow them into the deep water, and soon she found herself alone. She stood on one leg, then the other waiting for a fish to come by.

By now the Flamingo was so hungry that she decided any fish at all would do. "Even the tiniest minnow," she said.

But the Flamingo had lost her chance at having fish for breakfast. She finally had to settle for a tiny snail.

THOSE WHO ARE TOO CHOOSY MAY HAVE NO CHOICE IN THE END.

The Wolf and the Lamb

A young Lamb had strayed from her flock and was trying to find her way when a Wolf, who was hiding behind a tree, saw the Lamb coming.

"That Lamb will make a fine supper," the Wolf said to himself. "But I will need a good excuse for attacking one so young and innocent."

As soon as the Lamb neared the tree, the Wolf jumped out and shouted, "Do not take another step, for I remember you! You were the one eating grass in my part of the pasture the other day."

"It couldn't have been me!" said the Lamb. "I have never even tasted grass. I still drink my mother's milk."

"That may be," said the Wolf. "But it was you who said all those awful things about me last spring."

"Oh, no," said the Lamb. "I was not even born yet."

The Wolf grew angry and flustered. For the truth was, he was going to eat this Lamb whether he had reason to or not!

"Well, if you weren't born yet," said the Wolf, "it must have been your father who said awful things about me. And that is all the reason I need!"

Then the Wolf jumped upon the Lamb and that was the end of that.

THOSE WHO ARE OUT TO HURT YOU WILL USE ANY EXCUSE.

The Milkmaid

Early one morning a young Maiden was carrying a pail of milk to market when she got to thinking.

"This milk should bring me a good price. I am sure I will get enough money to buy a fine hen. I will take the hen home, where she will lay the very best eggs. But I will not sell the eggs. Oh, no. I will wait until the hen hatches them."

Just then, the Maiden noticed a ditch in the road. She carefully walked around it, so she would not spill any of the milk. Then she picked up her thinking where she had left off.

"Of course, the very best eggs will produce the very best chicks. I will feed and care for them. When they are grown, I will take the

and Her Pail

chickens to the market and sell them. Then I can buy the prettiest dress in town. I will wear that dress to the fair, and *all* boys will take notice of me. But I won't need to pay any attention to them. Why, I'll just lift up my head and . . ."

With that, the young Maiden lifted her head and the pail of milk came tumbling down. The Maiden was covered with milk, and her pail was empty. And with no milk to sell, there would be no hen and no chicks.

It was then that she remembered something her mother had told her:

DON'T COUNT YOUR CHICKS BEFORE THEY ARE HATCHED.

The Fox and the Goat

One day Fox fell into a deep well and could not get out. He had been trapped there for hours when a thirsty Goat came along.

"What are you doing down there?" asked Goat when she saw Fox at the bottom.

Fox had to think fast. "Haven't you heard?" he asked. "There is going to be a long dry spell, so I am drinking all the water I can." Fox slurped up the water noisily. "Ahh, delicious," he said. "Won't you come down and have some?"

"Thanks for asking," said Goat. And she jumped into the well.

Just as she was beginning to drink, Fox said, as though thinking it for the very first time, "Oh, my, I do believe we are stuck down here!"

Goat stopped drinking. "What will we do?" she cried.

"Here's the plan," said Fox. "If you place your feet against this wall, I will climb up your back and out of the well. Then, when I am free, I will help you get out."

Goat did as she was told. Fox jumped onto her back and then, pulling himself up by Goat's long horns, he made it out to safety. As soon as he was out, he turned and said, "Silly goat! If you had as many brains in your head as hairs in your beard you would have known better than to listen to someone in trouble." Then he raced away.

And there was Goat at the bottom of the well with plenty of time to think. If ever you should see her, this is what she'll tell you:

LOOK BEFORE YOU LEAP.

The Bundle of Sticks

One evening, a Father who was about to set off on a long journey gathered his children together and said, "There is something important I want you to know. But rather than tell you in words, I will show you what I mean."

The Father handed a bundle of sticks to his Eldest Son.

"I want you to break this bundle of sticks in two," he said.

"Yes, Father," said the Eldest Son. He took the bundle in his hands and, with a mighty effort, tried to break the sticks. Again and again he tried. But he could not do it.

"It is no use, Father," he said. "I cannot break the bundle in two."

"Pass the bundle to your Sister and let her try," the Father said.

The Sister took her turn trying to break the bundle of sticks, but could not do it either.

"Now let your youngest brother try," said their Father.

The Youngest Son tried as hard as the others, but it was no use. He could not break the bundle in two, so he handed it back to his Father.

The Father untied the bundle and gave one stick to each of his children. "See if you can break the sticks now," he said.

Of course, the sticks broke easily.

"Have I made myself clear?" asked the Father.

"Yes," said the Youngest Son. "If we stand together like the bundle of sticks, we will be strong."

"But if we become divided and stand alone," continued the Sister, "we can easily be broken."

The Eldest Son said it this way:

IN UNION THERE IS STRENGTH.

The Shepherd Boy

One day a Shepherd Boy was watching over his sheep when he got to thinking it would be nice to have company. Though all was peaceful in the pasture, the Boy stood up and cried, "Wolf! Wolf!" Then he sat back and waited.

Sure enough, the Villagers came running. "We're here to help! Where's the Wolf?" they called.

The boy laughed and said, "I was only fooling. There is no Wolf. I just wanted company."

The Villagers were angry at being tricked. "You won't have our company today!" they said. "We have more important things to tend to." And they hurried back down the hill.

and the Wolf

The next day the boy was at it again. "Wolf! Wolf!" he cried, just like before.

Again the Villagers came running. "You'll be sorry," they warned when they found the Boy had been lying.

That afternoon, a Wolf came out of nowhere. "Wolf! Wolf!" the Boy cried. "I mean it! There really is a Wolf!"

But this time, no one came. The Villagers heard the Boy calling, but they thought he was lying again. So the Wolf went in among the Boy's sheep and slaughtered them all.

IF YOU ARE IN THE HABIT OF LYING, NO ONE WILL BELIEVE YOU EVEN WHEN YOU TELL THE TRUTH.

The Gnat and the Bull

A tiny Gnat had flown a great distance and was feeling quite tired. So when he saw a Bull grazing in a field, he considered stopping on his horn for a short rest.

He hovered above the Bull for a moment, thinking, "I hope I won't be too much of a bother to him. First there's the matter of my weight. Then, too, I may find myself panting a bit because I'm so tired and the noise could trouble him. And if by any chance he has ticklish horns my tiny feet could drive him mad."

But the Gnat was so tired that he had no choice but to drop down onto the Bull's horn. The Bull didn't even blink an eye. "He really is being very gracious," thought the Gnat as he rested. "I must thank him before I leave."

As soon as he felt ready to continue his journey, the Gnat spoke up. "Ahem," he said importantly. "I want to thank you for having me as a guest on your horn. I hope I did not trouble you too much. And now I promise to be on my way."

"Go or stay," said the Bull matter-of-factly. "It's all the same to me. I didn't even notice you were there in the first place."

"Is that so!" said the outraged Gnat. He gave the Bull's horn a good hard kick.

Of course, the Bull didn't even notice.

WE ARE NOT ALWAYS AS IMPORTANT AS WE THINK WE ARE.

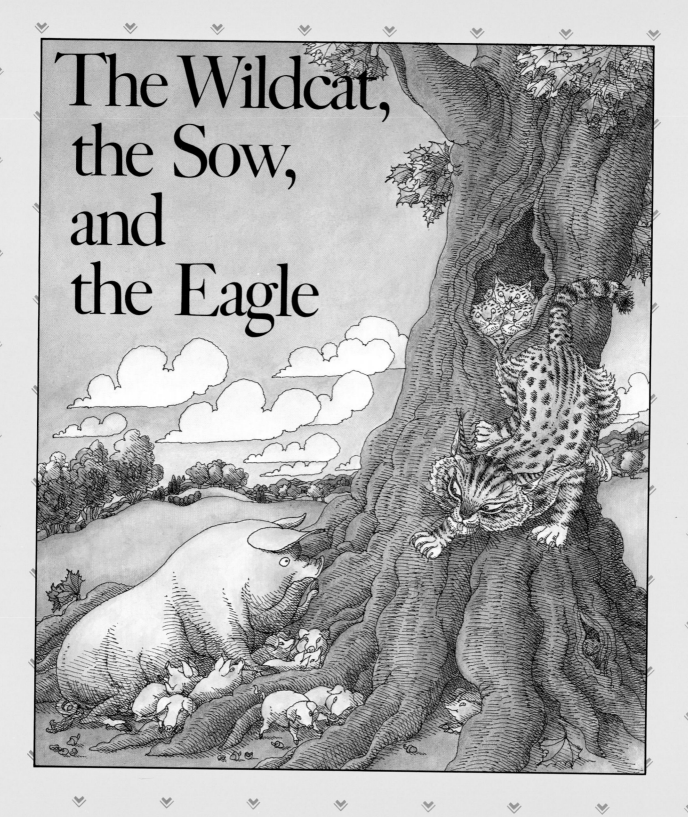

The Wildcat, the Sow, and the Eagle

Once three families made their homes in the same oak tree: An eagle set her nest in the top branches and hatched her chicks there. A wildcat made a den for her kittens in the hollow trunk. A sow dug a trench down among the roots and settled there with her piglets. How is that for an unlikely set of neighbors?

Well, they all got along fine, until the Wildcat decided to make some trouble. First she went to visit the Sow.

"Psst, Mrs. Sow!" called the Wildcat. "I have something to tell you."

"Don't be such a stranger," said the Sow. "Please, come in and sit down."

"Oh, no," said the Wildcat, "I can't stay. But I wanted to tell you that you'd better watch out for the Eagle that lives at the top of our tree. I heard her promising her chicks pork for dinner."

The Sow gasped. "Thank you for telling me!" she said. "I won't leave my piglets alone for a second."

The Wildcat visited the Eagle next. She made sure to stay several branches down, not wanting to make the Eagle nervous.

"Yoo-hoo!" called the Wildcat. "Mrs. Eagle, could you come out here for a moment?"

"Of course, Mrs. Wildcat," said the Eagle. "What can I do for you?"

"Well," said the Wildcat, "I wanted to ask you to join me in keeping an eye on that Sow who lives downstairs. I notice she's been digging deeper and deeper into our roots, and I'm afraid this whole tree is going to come crashing down at any time."

"My word!" said the Eagle. "I will certainly keep an eye on her and if I feel the slightest tremor I'll call you right away."

"I knew I could count on you," said the Wildcat and she returned to her den.

Naturally, the Sow and the Eagle were beside themselves with worry. Neither was willing to leave her young alone, even to go hunting.

But each night, as soon as the others fell asleep, the Wildcat sneaked

off and got the best food for her kittens. This went on for weeks. The Sow family and the Eagle family would have starved for sure if the Wildcat had not been tracked down one night and killed by hunters.

It was only then that the Eagle and the Sow met face to face. Hearing the kittens mewing, they each sneaked away to care for them.

"How could you!" shouted the Sow when she saw the Eagle. "How could you even think of having my little piglets for supper!"

"Why, I would never dream of such a thing," said the Eagle. "But you! You go on digging and digging at the roots of this tree when you know very well it could come toppling down and my chicks don't

even know how to fly!" With that, the Eagle broke down in tears.

"I don't dig at the roots," said the Sow. "Our home is quite comfortable just as it is. I would never do anything that could harm your chicks."

"Then that Wildcat was just a nasty old gossip!" said the Eagle.

"Yes," said the Sow. "But still someone must care for these poor little kittens."

And so the Eagle and the Sow put the words of the Wildcat behind them and became close friends.

NEVER TRUST A GOSSIP.

The Frog and the Ox

"I want to leap first this time," said the Frog to her Brother.

"You leaped first this morning. It's my turn," her Brother said.

Suddenly they stopped their bickering and gazed into the meadow, where something huge and horrible had appeared.

"Let's get out of here!" shouted Brother Frog. They hopped toward home as fast as they could to tell their family what they had seen. Along the way they met their Uncle.

"Where are you racing?" he asked. "You look like you've just seen a ghost."

"No, it was a monster!" croaked the Brother. "And it was bigger than anything we've ever seen. It had horns on its head!"

"And it had a long tail and hoofs that were split in two!" croaked the sister.

"Now, now," said their Uncle. "That was no monster. It was only an Ox. I've seen many an Ox in my day, and they really aren't so huge. Why, I could easily make myself as big."

Uncle Frog blew himself up and asked, "Was he this big?"

"Oh, no, Uncle," croaked the young Frogs. "The Ox was much bigger."

"Oh, was he," said Uncle Frog. He blew himself up some more. "Now am I as big?" he asked.

"You're not even close," croaked the Young Frogs. "But don't worry about it. You don't have to be as big as the Ox."

"It's no problem!" shouted their Uncle. But this time when he blew himself up—he burst!

WHEN YOU TRY TO BE SOMETHING YOU'RE NOT, YOU END UP BEING NOTHING AT ALL.

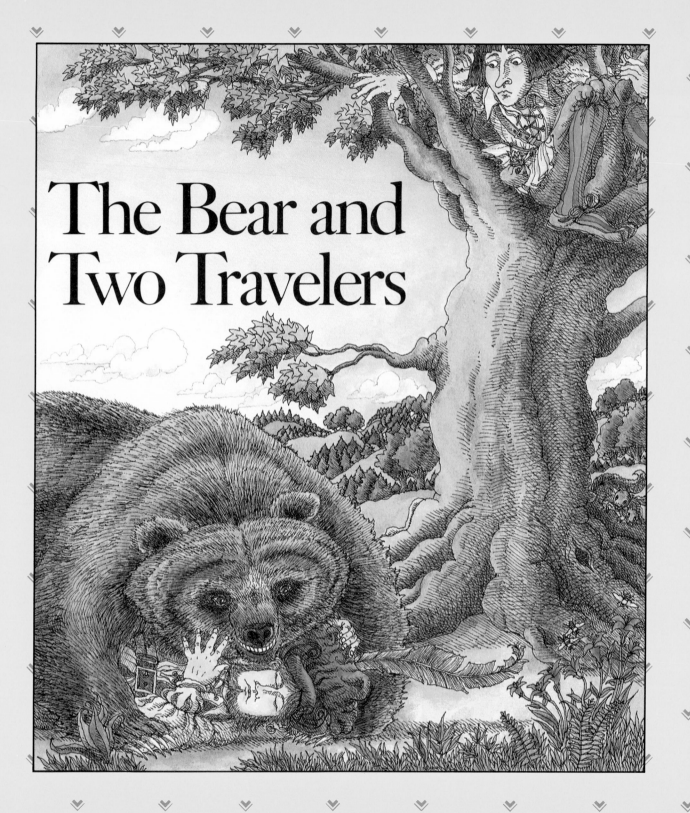

The Bear and Two Travelers

"What a great day!" said the First Traveler to his friend.

"It sure is," said the Second Traveler. "We picked the perfect day for a hike in the woods."

The Second Traveler took a deep breath of fresh air. But his breath turned into a gasp when he saw who was heading their way. It was a large brown bear. The Second Traveler scampered up the nearest tree. Only then did he bother to warn his friend that the Bear was coming.

By the time the First Traveler saw the Bear, he had no chance to run for cover. So he dropped down to the ground and played dead.

He was lying there trying not to tremble, when the Bear walked up to him and began to sniff. The First Traveler felt the Bear's hot, moist breath on his face.

"Pshew!" he thought. "This Bear must have eaten some bad fish."

Then the Bear started swaying from side to side, making strange gurgling noises deep in his throat. The Traveler was sure the end was near.

But he was wrong. The Bear thought the Traveler was dead and it is said that a Bear will not touch a dead body. So the Bear left.

He was long gone and far away, when the Second Traveler came down from his hiding place in the tree.

"I guess I should have warned you the Bear was coming," said the Second Traveler. "But I wanted to make sure I was safe first. You understand, don't you?"

"No," said the First Traveler, "I don't."

"Anyway, I saw that Bear whispering sweet nothings in your ear," the Second Traveler said teasingly. "What did he have to say?"

"He told me something very wise," the First Traveler said.

"Really?" asked the Second Traveler, "What was that?"

"Next time you see him," said the First Traveler, "ask him yourself!" And he turned and walked away.

Now we all know that bears can't talk. But if this one could have, he would have said this:

A FRIEND WHO LEAVES YOU IN TIME OF NEED, IS NO FRIEND AT ALL.

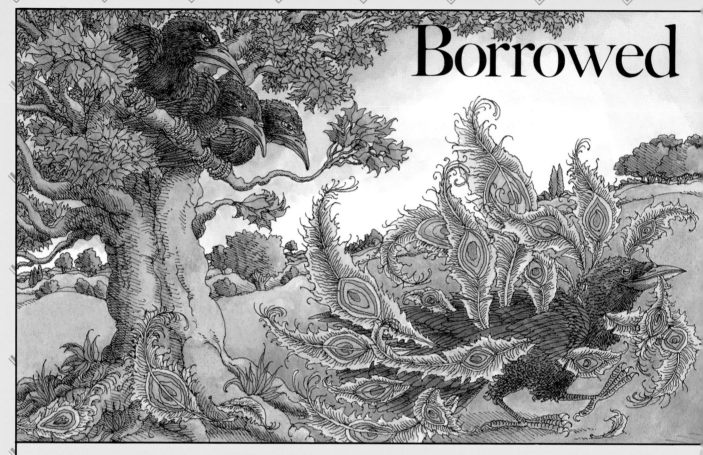

Borrowed

A Crow was out walking one morning when he saw a family of peacocks traveling just ahead of him. Behind them, they left a trail of beautiful feathers.

"Look at all the colors!" thought Crow to himself. "I'm tired of being a common, colorless bird. If I had feathers like those I'd be a fine bird, too."

So he followed their trail, gathering up as many of the feathers as he could carry in his beak. Then he sneaked behind the bushes and covered himself with the peacock feathers as best he could. When the last feather was in place, he lifted his head up high and strutted off to join the peacocks!

But the peacocks were no fools. Even the littlest one started to

Feathers

giggle when she saw the silly Crow. "Look, Mommy," she said. "That bird is playing dress-up!"

The others did not think the trick very funny. "Who do you think you're fooling?" they asked. "We'll just take our feathers and you can go back where you came from!" They pecked away at the Crow until they had every one of their feathers back.

The trembling Crow flew off to find his family. But when he got home, he found no welcome there either. "We saw what you did," they told him. "Do you think we're not good enough for you?"

Then they turned their backs on the sorry bird, speaking just loud enough for him to overhear:

FINE FEATHERS DO NOT MAKE FINE BIRDS.

The Fox and the Grapes

One hot summer day Fox sat down to rest awhile in the shade of a leafy tree. He had just settled back against the trunk when he looked up and saw a glistening bunch of grapes twisting through the branches overhead.

"This is my lucky day!" Fox said. "I am thirsty and those grapes look cool and juicy."

Fox stood up to pick some of the grapes, but at first try he could not reach them. He tried again, standing up on the tips of his toes and stretching as far as he could. Still, he could not touch the grapes.

"Those grapes are higher than I had thought," said Fox.

So he jumped way up and swatted at them, but that didn't work either.

By now Fox's tongue was hanging out of his mouth, for he was thirstier than ever. Then he had an idea. "I am sure this will work," he thought.

Fox found a big rock nearby and inch by inch—for the rock was heavy—he pushed it under the grapes. Then he stood upon the rock, and once again reached up as far as he could. But poor Fox just fell from the rock empty handed.

Fox dusted himself off and continued down the road. He only looked back once to say, "Who needs those grapes anyway? I am sure they are sour."

IT IS EASY TO DISLIKE WHAT YOU CANNOT HAVE.

The Dog in the Manger

Once a mean Old Dog who was tired of yipping and yapping and chasing the chickens around, decided to take a rest. Looking for a quiet spot, he came across a manger and jumped into it. As he did, he got some hay in his mouth and had to spit it out.

"Phooey!" he said. "I don't see how any animal could eat this. It's dry and tasteless." Then, the Dog settled down and went to sleep. He would have been better off without the scratchy hay beneath him, but he was too lazy to get rid of it.

Later, after a long day's work, three Oxen came to the manger to eat some of the hay that had been put there for them. The Old Dog was awakened by the sound of their approaching hoofs and began to bark angrily, "Go away! Can't you see I'm sleeping?"

"But we're hungry," said the first Ox.

"Get up and let us have our supper," begged the second.

The Dog stayed where he was and went on barking.

"Why, you don't even want to eat that hay," said the third tired Ox. "And it can't be very comfortable. But still you won't let us near it. You're just mean."

To show how mean he was, the Dog barked one last time at the Oxen, then went right back to sleep on their supper.

ONLY THE MEANEST CREATURES WOULD KEEP FROM OTHERS THINGS THEY CANNOT EVEN USE THEMSELVES.

The Miller, His Son,

"Come along," said the Miller to his Son. "We don't want to be late to the fair."

The fair was in a neighboring town and the Miller and his Son were going to sell their Donkey for the best price they could get.

"I'm coming," said the Miller's Son, pulling the Donkey behind him.

They hadn't gone very far when they passed a well where a group of women were whispering to one another. Now, who do you think they were whispering about? That's right. The Miller, his Son, and the Donkey.

"How silly that man is," said one of the women, just loud enough

and the Donkey

to be overheard. "Why in the world is he walking when he has a donkey he could ride?"

"Now that," said the Miller, "is a good question."

The Miller was happy to continue walking, but he lifted his Son onto the Donkey and they went on their way.

They had not gone far when they met a group of old men standing by the roadside, talking. And who do you think they were talking about? That's right. The Miller, his Son, and the Donkey.

"Look at that," said the eldest of the group. "There's a perfect example of what I've been saying. The young have no respect for their elders anymore. That healthy young boy is riding while his

father walks the long, dusty road."

"Yes, indeed!" shouted the embarrassed Miller to his Son. "How dare you ride when I am walking. Get down at once!"

"But, but . . ." said the Miller's Son, who was quite puzzled since his father had put him up there in the first place.

"I don't want any backtalk," said the Miller. Then he climbed up onto the Donkey, leaving his son to walk alongside.

Just around the bend they met a group of women and children. Suddenly, one of the women began to shout. And who do you think she was shouting about? That's right. The Miller, his Son, and the Donkey.

"You're a cruel, cruel man!" she cried. "How can you let a poor helpless boy walk this stony path while you sit up there like a king! Shame on you!"

The Miller hung his head. "Of course she is right, dear Son. I don't know what got into me." The Miller quickly scooped his son up onto the Donkey with him.

They had almost reached the town when they were stopped by a man, shaking his head and pointing his finger. And who do you think he was pointing at? That's right. The Miller, his Son, and the Donkey.

"How could you be so mean," he said, "to load up a poor beast up that way. Why, there are two of you and only one of him. You should be carrying that Donkey, not riding him!"

The Miller slapped his hand to his forehead. "I can't believe myself," he moaned. "And you, Son. Didn't you know any better either?"

The Miller and his Son jumped down and tied the legs of the Donkey together with heavy cord. Then they turned the Donkey upside down, rested the cord on a pole, and started over the bridge to town.

They were halfway across the bridge when a crowd of people descended upon them. The people were roaring with laughter. And who do you think they were laughing at? That's right. The Miller, his Son, and the Donkey.

"That must be some special Donkey!" they cried. "I should have it so good!"

The people clapped their hands and stamped their feet, delighted with the silly show. This did not please the Donkey. He was already uncomfortable riding upside down, and now the noise was making him nervous. He began to squirm, trying to get free. Sure enough, the cords that held him broke and the Donkey fell down into the river.

"Woe is me," said the Miller. "How did this all happen?"

Well, Mr. Miller . . .

WHEN YOU TRY TO PLEASE EVERYONE, YOU PLEASE NO ONE AT ALL.

The Goose who Laid the Golden Eggs

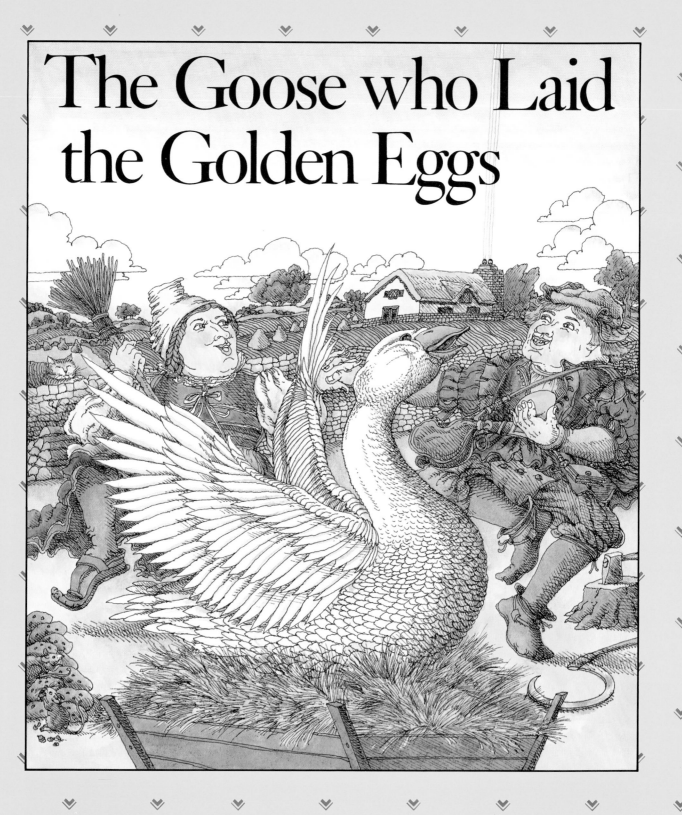

Early one morning a Farmer went to the nest of his Goose for an egg. When he looked inside the nest, he saw an egg that was like none he had ever laid eyes on before. It was shimmering gold. He picked it up. It was heavy. The egg was solid gold through and through.

"Wifey! Wifey!" he called. "Our Goosey has laid a golden egg for us!"

"Fancy that," said the Farmer's Wife. "Can I wear it around my neck?"

"You could, but your neck might break from the weight of it. It's solid gold!"

The Farmer's Wife felt how heavy the egg was and cried, "We're rich!"

Then the Farmer and his Wife joined hands and danced round and round the old kitchen table.

They did not have that old table for long. With the money they got from selling the egg, they went out and had an expensive new table made for themselves.

Each morning there was another golden egg waiting for them. And each day, the Farmer and his Wife sold the egg and bought something new.

One morning, the Farmer spotted the Goose as she was leaving her nest. Again, she had left him a glimmering gold egg. But the Farmer had become greedy and thought, "Why should I settle for just one egg each day? I'll open her up and take them all at once!"

So he chased his Goose round the farm until he caught her and killed her, and opened her up. But there were no eggs inside her. And now his good Goose was gone.

The Farmer stamped his feet and shook his fists to the sky for his foolishness.

THOSE WHO ARE TOO GREEDY END UP WITH NOTHING.

Belling the Cat

There once was a family of mice who lived happily in a small house in the country. But one day a Cat moved in. As a hunter of mice, he was silent and quick.

"Why just yesterday, if I hadn't been warned by his shadow, that Cat would have eaten me!" cried a Young Mouse.

The Young Mouse's mother gathered her son in her arms. "We will call a meeting," she said. "We must do something about that Cat!"

And so there was a meeting of the mice. The Old Mouse was the first to speak.

"Our main problem is that the Cat is so quiet. We need to hear him coming so we have time to escape. We must develop a warning system."

"Yes, yes, that is right," said the other mice in agreement. Then the

room grew silent as they began to think. The only sound to be heard was the tap-tap-tapping of tiny tails on the floor.

At last someone spoke up. It was the Young Mouse. "I know what to do!" he said. "We'll hang a bell around the cat's neck. We can tie it on with a piece of ribbon. That way, when the Cat is near, we will hear the bell ringing and can run for cover."

"Bravo!!" shouted the other mice. "It's a brilliant idea."

The Young Mouse's mother was especially proud. The Old Mouse was the only one not cheering. "And who among you is going to put this bell around the Cat's neck?" he asked.

Once again the only sound to be heard was the tap-tap-tapping of tiny tails.

SOME THINGS ARE EASIER SAID THAN DONE.

AESOP

was, according to legend, a slave on the Greek Island of Samos in the sixteenth century B.C. It is said that he was an exceptionally ugly and misshapen man. Yet he was a brilliant storyteller, who may have used these fables, which most often depict animal characters acting and speaking like human beings, to make statements about the rulers of his time. Whether fact or fiction, Aesop is credited with almost all the fables we know today. And the morals are as true now as they ever were.

STEPHANIE CALMENSON

is the author of many books for children, including *Fido* and *What Am I?*, and she is the compiler, with Joanna Cole, of *The Laugh Book:* A New Treasury of Humor for Children, and *The Read-Aloud Treasury.* Before turning to writing full-time, she was an elementary school teacher, a children's book editor, and editorial director of *Parents' Magazine*'s Read-Aloud Book Club for Children. She grew up in Brooklyn, New York, and now lives in Manhattan.

ROBERT BYRD

illustrator of several books for children, has had his work exhibited at the Philadelphia Art Alliance, the Society of Illustrators, the Bologna Children's Book Fair, and the Children's Book Showcase. He teaches at the Philadelphia Colleges of the Arts in Philadelphia.

Quality Printing and Binding by:
Horowitz/Rae Book Manufacturers, Inc.
300 Fairfield Road
Fairfield, NJ 07006 U.S.A.